The Nutquacker

written and illustrated by

MARY JANE AUCH

SCHOLASTIC INC.

New York Toronto London Auckland Sydney
Mexico City New Delhi Hong Kong Buenos Aires

CLARA was a farm duck
and this was her first winter.
One morning, she noticed the older
farm animals whispering together.

"Coooool it!" mooed the cow
when Clara came near.

"I won't say-hay-hay-ay another
word," whinnied the horse.

"Just go ba-a-a-ack to your pond,"
the sheep bleated to Clara. "We have
pla-a-a-ans to make."

Over the next few days, Clara tried
to eavesdrop. She didn't hear much,
but one word came up over and over.
"I know your secret!" Clara told the
horse. "It's Christmas!"

The horse only smiled.

"So . . . what exactly is Christmas?" Clara asked. "Will you show me?"

"Try to be pay-hay-hay-hatient," whinnied the horse. "You'll find out."

Clara wasn't very good at being patient. "I can't wait. Will you take me to Christmas, Horse?"

"I never travel far from my own neigh-neigh-neighborhood," whinnied the horse. "Just stay here on the farm and way-hay-hay-hait."

"But I want to go now!" Clara insisted. "How about you, Cow? Will you help me find Christmas?"

"No, Christmas will come sooooon enough," mooed the cow. "Besides, all that moooooving around might turn my milk to milkshakes."

"What about you, Sheep?" asked Clara. "Won't you join me in a wild and woolly search for Christmas?"

"This is a ba-a-a-a-ad time to go wandering off," bleated the sheep. "I ca-a-a-a-an't leave right now."

"You'd rather stand around doing nothing?
You're all crazy!" quacked Clara.
"We're not cray-hay-hay-hazy," whinnied the horse.
"You're the looooony one," mooed the cow.
"You're a nutty duck, a real
nutqu-a-a-a-acker!" bleated the sheep.

"Nutquacker! Nutquacker!" teased the pig,
who was usually the butt of jokes himself.
    "Every one of you is a stick-in-the-mud,"
mumbled Clara. "I'll go find Christmas all alone."
As she set off, it began to snow.

It snowed harder as Clara trudged along. She brushed the snowflakes from her beak and kept waddling until she came to a tall mountain. "I'll be able to see the whole world from the top of that mountain," she said. "That's how I'll find Christmas."

Clara struggled until she reached the very top. "I made it!" she cried.

A giant monster with huge eyes waited in the field ahead of her.

"Christmas must be hidden behind those trees in the distance. I can't turn back just because a giant monster with huge eyes is blocking my path. I may be small, but I'm smart. I'll find a way to get by him."

Clara slid down the other side of the mountain, gathered up her courage, and walked right up to the monster. "Watch out, Monster," she quacked. "I might look like an ordinary duck, but if you try to hurt me, I'll make you disappear."

The monster didn't move an inch. He didn't even blink.

Clara smiled. "Wise choice, Monster. You don't touch me. I don't zap you."

Clara circled the monster, just to prove how brave she was. Then she waddled on across the field, pleased with her cleverness.

But it wasn't long before a new danger loomed ahead.

"A large animal with sharp horns," Clara quacked. "No problem. If I could fool a giant monster with huge eyes, a large animal with sharp horns should be easy to trick." As she drew closer, Clara yelled, "Back off, large animal!"

Before Clara could say another word, the animal ran away. "I'm getting good at this," Clara said, "but I'm tired, hungry, and cold and I still haven't found Christmas."

Clara hadn't traveled far before something else blocked her path.

"A small creature with soft fur," Clara quacked. "Piece of cake. If I could outwit a giant monster with huge eyes and a large animal with sharp horns, a small creature with soft fur won't stop me from finding Christmas. Be careful, small creature!" Clara drew closer.

The creature didn't run away.

"I may look like an ordinary duck," Clara quacked, "but I'm powerful. If you touch even as much as one of my feathers, I'll turn you into a pile of dust."

The creature didn't move a hair.

"Way to go," Clara said, as she waddled past him.

"You don't hurt me. I don't pulverize you."

Suddenly, Clara felt a sharp pain in the tail feathers. She whirled around.

"I'm touching feathers here," said the creature. "Do I look like a pile of dust to you?"

"Don't talk with your mouth full," Clara said, thinking fast. "I've stopped a giant monster with huge eyes. I've scared off a large animal with sharp horns. No small creature can stand in my way."

The creature's eyes narrowed. "Then I won't stand. I'll pounce!"

Just as the creature lunged for Clara, the feathers tickled his nose. He started to sneeze, giving Clara the chance she needed to escape. She waddled for dear life through the falling darkness, listening to the sneezing fit behind her.

But Clara knew that when the sneezing stopped, the creature would come after her.

Finally, Clara had to stop to catch her breath. She hid under some low-hanging branches, hoping the creature wouldn't discover her. "Why did I ever leave the farm and my friends?" she whimpered. "I'd give anything to be with them now. But I've come so far, I don't know how to find my way back."

Then she noticed a light cutting through the
darkness ahead. Was it shelter or a new danger?
Though she knew it was risky, Clara left the protection
of her hiding place. "That light is my only hope,"
she gasped. She waddled toward it at full speed.

Clara heard the creature closing in behind her.
She gathered her last bit of strength and plunged
through the drifting snow.

Clara burst through a door
and found herself in a magical
but familiar place.

All of her farm friends were there. "I'm home!"
she cried. "I'm so glad to see you. I must have been
walking in a big circle the whole time."

"Clara's ba-a-a-ack!" bleated the sheep.

"Just in time to celebray-hay-hay-ate Christmas!"
whinnied the horse.

"With lots of delicious foooood!" mooed the cow.

The pigs didn't say anything. They were too busy eating.

"We couldn't tell you we were
pla-a-a-anning a surprise Christmas
party," bleated the sheep. "We made you
a special present. It's a nutqua-a-a-acker."

"Just for yooooou,"
mooed the cows.

Clara hugged the nutquacker.
"I love it. I'm sorry I was so
mean before."

From then on, the animals
danced the night away.

"So Christmas is treats and dancing and getting presents?" asked Clara.

"Christmas is giving, tooooo!"
mooed the cows.

"Tha-a-a-t's not all," bleated
the sheep. "Christmas is being with
the ones who love you."

As the party
drew to a close,
Clara looked around
at all of her friends.
She was already
thinking of Christmas
gifts to make for
them next year.

For Kera,
Welcome
to the Auch
family

ISBN 0-439-47323-3

12 11 10 9 8 7 6 5 4 3 2 1   2 3 4 5 6 7/0

Printed in the U.S.A.   14

First Scholastic printing, December 2002

Book design by Sylvia Frezzolini Severance